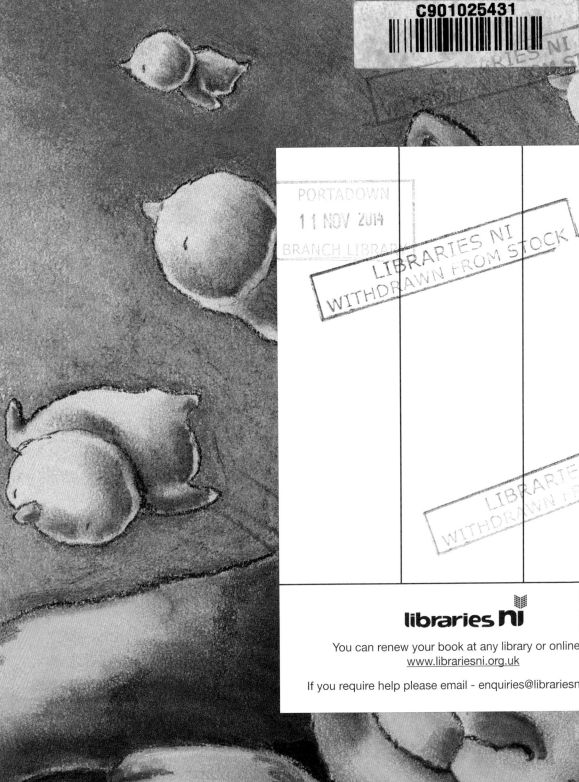

First published in 2014 by
Birlinn Limited
West Newington House
10 Newington Road
Edinburgh
EH9 1QS

www.birlinn.co.uk

ISBN: 978 1 78027 199 6

British Library Cataloguing-in-Publication Data
A catalogue record for this book is available from
the British Library

Printed and bound by Latimer Trend,
Plymouth

THE TOBERMORY CAT BY DEBI GLIORI 123

BIRLINN

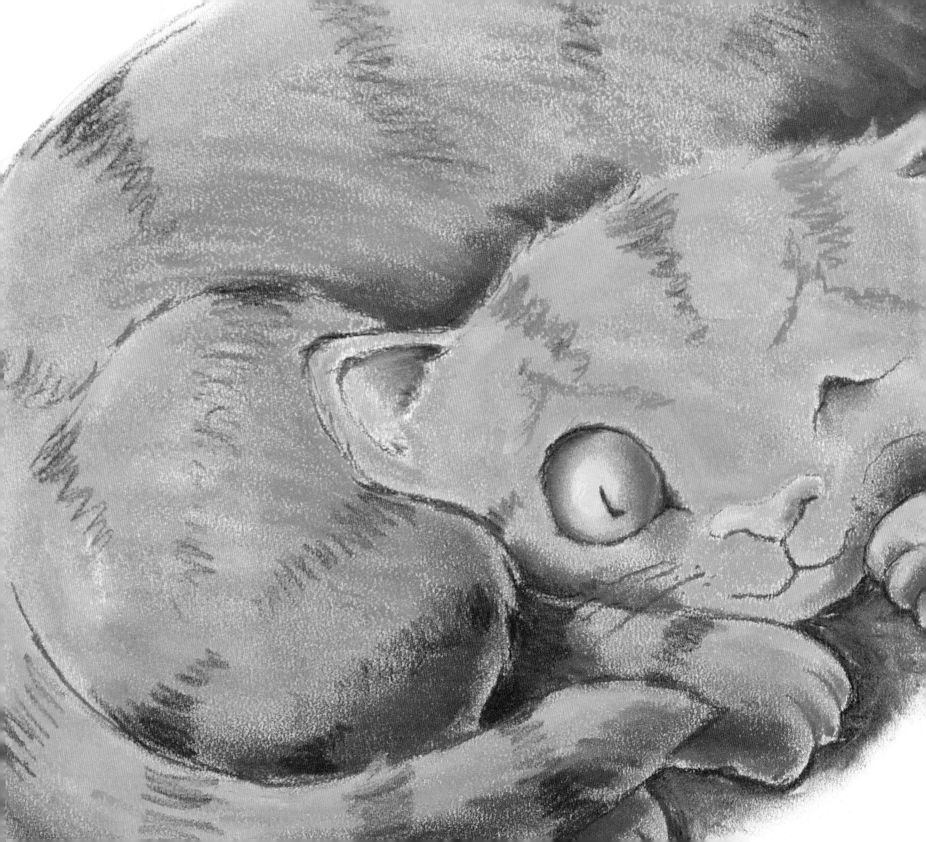

The Tobermory Cat
wakes up with
an empty tummy.

M I A O W W W

he wails,

F E E D   M E !

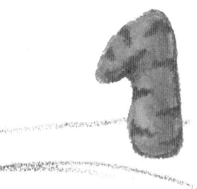

Breakfast is
one
bowl of cat food and
two
saucers
of milk.

But . . .
Tobermory Cat's
tummy is still empty.
Time to go a-hunting.
Three yachts sail past.

Three
people take his
photograph.

And third time lucky –
Tobermory Cat finds
three crab claws
on the pier.

Now for a nap. Tobermory Cat likes to sleep on top of cars.

But not just any old car. Tobermory Cat is very picky. Car number one is too big.

Car number two is too small.

Car number three
is full of dog breath . . .

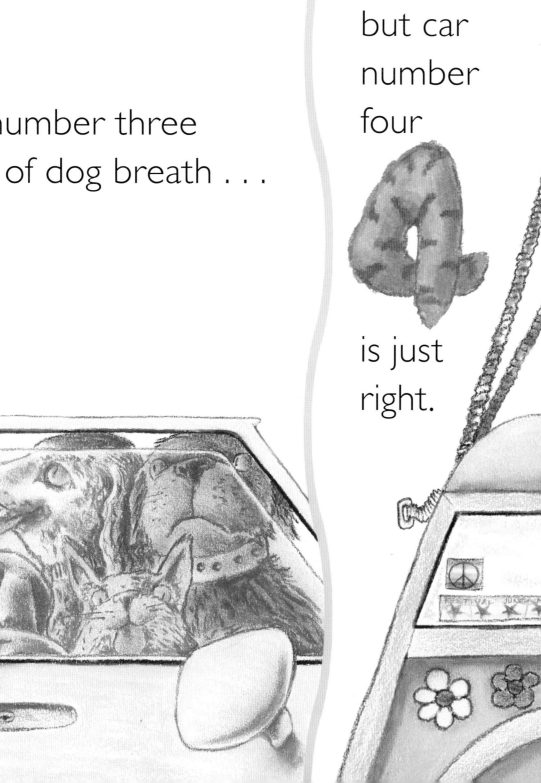

but car
number
four

is just
right.

When Tobermory Cat wakes up
it is time for lunch.

Time to visit his five S houses. YUM!

Tobermory Cat washes all four paws plus his tail, which makes five.

The kind bookshop
owner has something
to make the cat better.

Seven special salmon snacks.
Tobermory Cat is in heaven.

He falls fast asleep
and dreams he's eating
 eight birds, one after
the other.

(Fortunately
for the birds,
this is only
a dream.)

When Tobermory Cat wakes up,
dolphins are playing hide-and-seek
out in the bay. Tobermory Cat would love
to join in, but he hates swimming.
He yawns and nine 9 midges stick
to his tongue.
UGH!

Tobermory Cat has
a dinner date
at the Mishnish.
Cats aren't allowed
in the restaurant,
so he dines outside.

He has ten **10** fish all to himself. Now his tummy is very nearly full. There's just one thing missing . . .

But look – this is no ordinary puddle.
The night sky is reflected there.
All of the stars.
ONE, TWO, THREE,
A HUNDRED, A THOUSAND,
A MILLION, A BILLION,
A GALAXY,
A UNIVERSE . . .

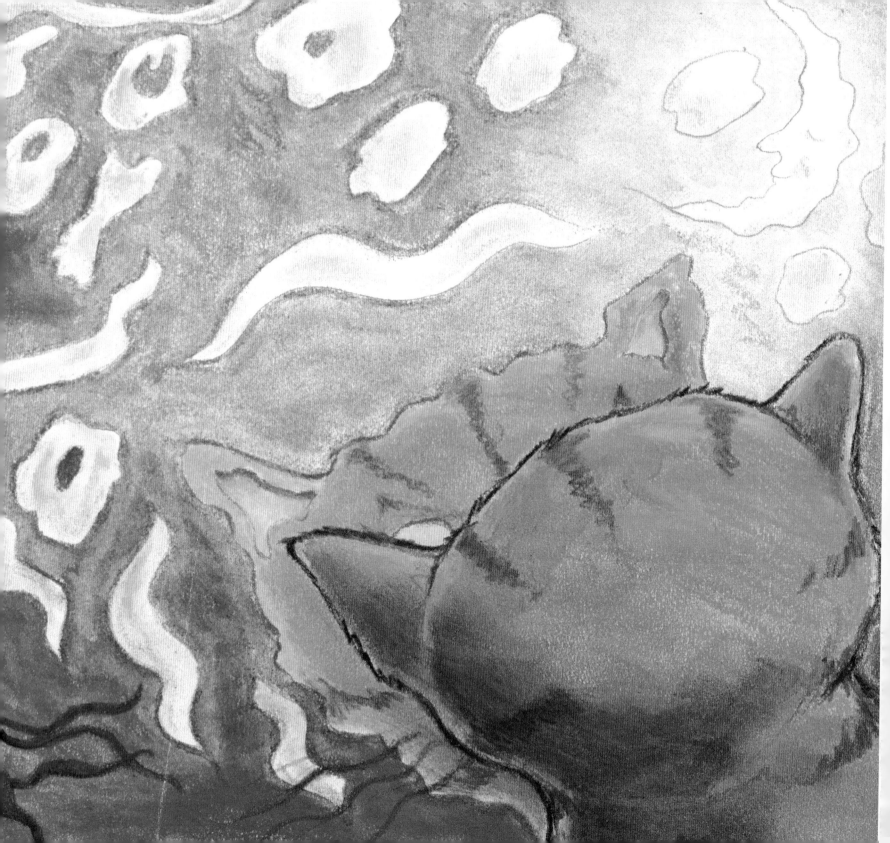

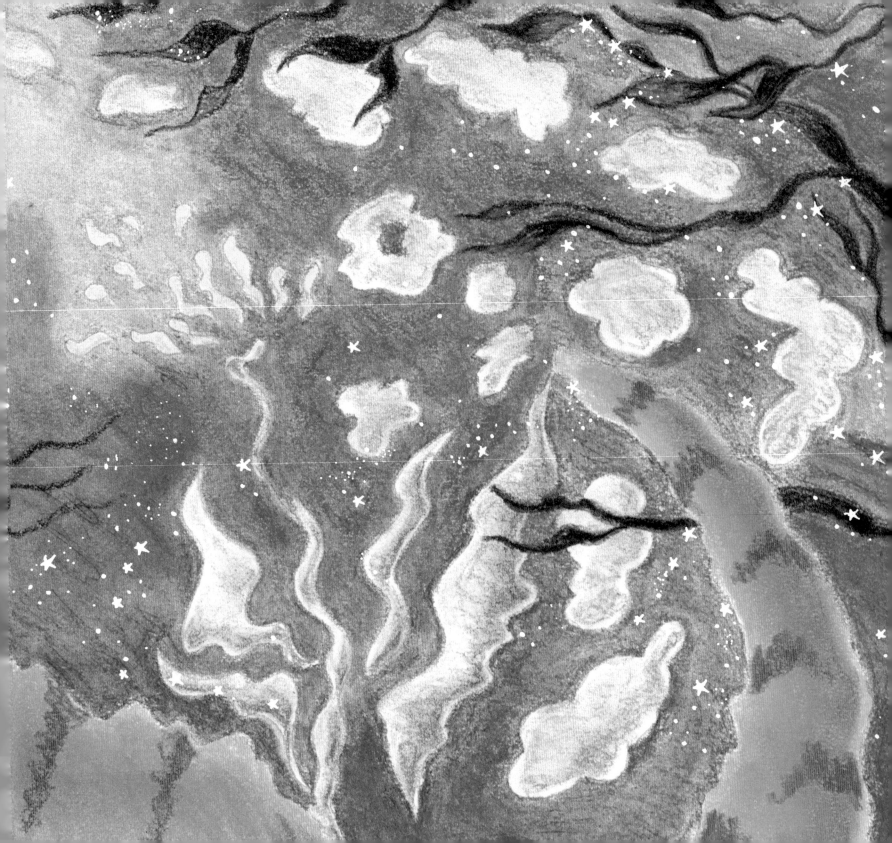

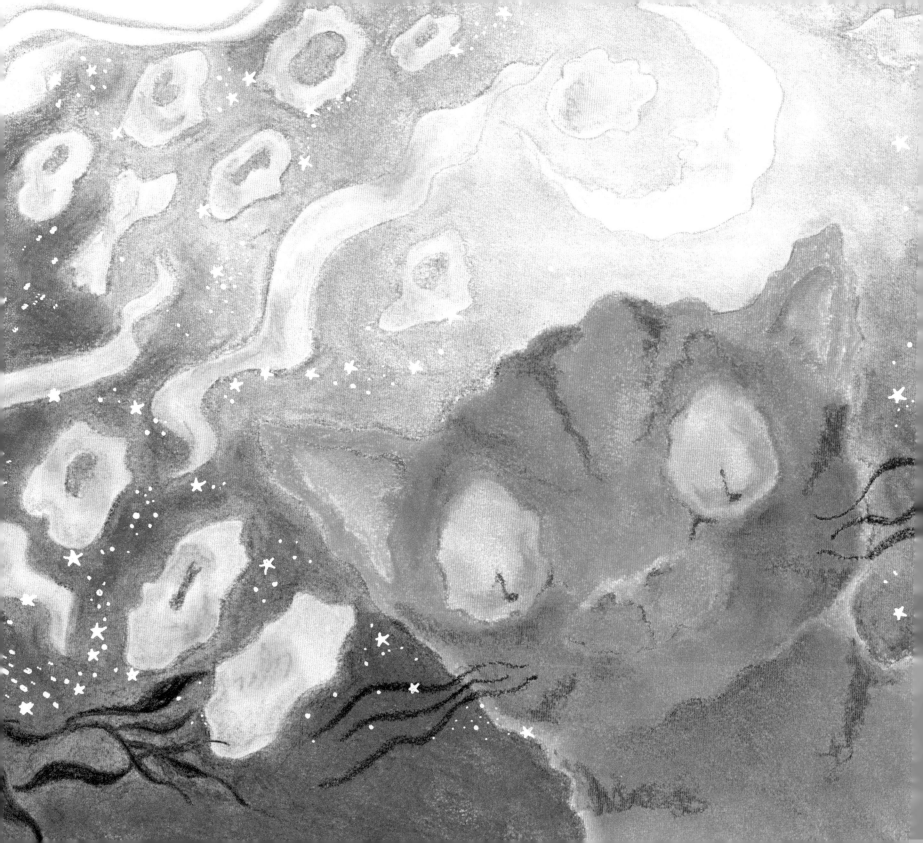

Lap, lap, lap
goes Tobermory Cat,
drinking up the night
until it is gone.

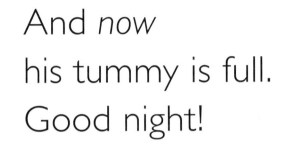

And *now*
his tummy is full.
Good night!